A Short Rhetoric for Leaving the Family

PETER DIMOCK

Library of Congress Cataloging-in-Publication Data:

Dimock, Peter, 1950-
    A short rhetoric for leaving the family : a novel / by Peter
Dimock. — 1st ed.
        p.   cm.
    ISBN 1-56478-210-7 (pb : alk. paper)
    1. Vietnamese Conflict, 1961-1975—United States—
Influence—Fiction. I. Title.
    PS3554.I4394S56   1998
    813'.54—dc21   92-22017
                                                CIP

This publication is partially supported by a grant from the Illinois
Arts Council, a state agency.

Dalkey Archive Press
Illinois State University
Campus Box 4241
Normal, IL 61790-4241

visit our website at: www.cas.ilstu.edu/english/dalkey/dalkey.html

for Nancy

Vir bonus, dicendi peritus—Marcus Cato (the Elder)
(The good man, skilled in speaking)

The office and duty of rhetoric is to apply reason to the imagination for the better moving of the will.
                                                    —Francis Bacon

This historical present made from speech: some speech for the pleasured man. Some German friend for an idea of it afterwards.
                    —Jarlath Lanham (from a notebook entry dated
                          19 March 1989, Father's 70th birthday)

Invention

Invention

———◆———

Dear Des and General,

This attempt at a reliable method of direct address is to be left with my lawyer and delivered to you on, or as soon as practicable after, 20 September 2001, when you will have reached the ages of twenty-one and twenty-two respectively. Along with this manuscript comes what I assume will, in eleven years time, be a considerable sum of money which I have divided equally between you. The principle in the trust I have established in your names is now a little over eight hundred and fifty thousand dollars. I expect it to have much more than doubled by the time you receive it.

My object is to provide you with the means, should you find it necessary as I now do, to leave the Lanham family. I begin to write this at the table from the room AG and I shared as children in the Maine summer house. I stripped and refinished it myself last spring. I have placed it here under the window in the front room of my apartment where I have been living quite successfully for the past eight months. The previous two and a half years I spent, as you may know, as a resident of the Conway Cooperative Care Center, a halfway house for assisted living. I give the staff and my co-residents there much of the credit for my recovery of a sense of wholeness in my life and of my present, grateful confidence in the course of action I have chosen. I will, in the not too distant future, leave here—not without trepidation—and move to the Midwest. I have applied for a position as an assistant to the educational director of a small but highly regarded nature center and natural history museum located on what was once a private estate adjacent to one of the largest remaining undivided tracts of conservation land in that part of the country.

I assume, in the wake of the incident on Hospital Hill two Thanksgivings ago—which I'm sure you yourselves clearly recall—that I will, in accordance with the terms of the court agreement, have no contact with either of you between now and the moment you attain your legal capacity to read these documents for yourselves and exercise your rights accordingly. In the meantime, I am perfectly aware that your Grandfather Lanham, AG, and Lena all will have communicated their belief that I seriously jeopardized your welfare that afternoon. I strongly dissent from the characterization of my behavior as endangerment, but have signed an agreement in the chambers of a family-court judge stating that I will have no further contact with you before you attain your legal majority. I did so as part of a settlement worked out by my lawyer in order to prevent further attempts by Father, AG, and the other family members they enlisted to put obstacles in the path of my assumption of complete responsibility for my own medical and psychiatric care.

The following pages do intimately concern the Lanham family history, but I hasten to assure you that they contain no revelations of family secrets. All the events and facts related here, I am sure, will already be known to you. They are, for the most part, matters of public record or easily available from any number of family members, close friends or disinterested witnesses. Furthermore, I have no doubt that the events recounted will go largely uncontested by the principals themselves. The purpose of my method is solely to provide you the means of leaving the family entirely, should you desire to do so—to provide you, in other words, some speech for another history. My sole concern is your welfare. I do not intend in any way to alienate you from those you love or to call into question their devotion or generosity towards you in pursuing what they consider the family's best interests. I speak to you as to sons I may never have.

Des, you will notice that I have taken the liberty of including you as a member of the Lanham family. I do so for rhetorical convenience and prolepsis: I am assigning to you fully one half of the family trust intended for me and future direct descendants of the Lanham line. I hope you will indulge my presumption. My intention is the exercise of good faith. I ask your forgiveness if there has been any failure of judgment on my part.

I write these words in late December in the year of our Lord 1990, as we all wait for the war in the Persian Gulf to begin. There is not the slightest doubt that the planes will fly and the bombs will fall. There is the usual excitement. Father, I gather, has been on constant call from the administration though his comings and goings remain discreetly off the record. I understand that he has even met with military planners of ground operations several times, and has privately briefed key members of the relevant Congressional committees in preparation for various closed-session hearings. His perspective is, needless to say, much in demand. I get the sense that there are to be no mistakes this time—on anyone's part. There is a professionalism and rehearsed polish to everything. As a public we seem both taken by surprise by this war and excited in some abstract way.

Father and AG are working eighteen-hour days. AG's advice as an experienced Defense Department intelligence analyst is much sought after, of course. He is highly regarded in decision-making circles for studies he has directed on civilian mobilization in Islamic cultures. I get all this information from Anna when I visit her on Wednesdays—often just overhearing her on the phone with friends at the college. Despite the sensitivity to security you might suppose she would have developed in those years of marriage to Father, she can't seem to resist letting people know how important her ex-husband and son are.

I assume this will sound quite strange to you, reading it from your present vantage point, but my method is intended to accommodate, and sometimes even exploit, the liabilities of distance. What truly matters is keeping in mind a certain directness of speech that my method is at some pains both to demonstrate and to propose.

At this writing, Lena is still teaching at Salisbury College in the political science department. Anna (even as you are reading this) will probably still be teaching in the English department. Lena has refused to participate in a college colloquium on the coming war sponsored by an ad hoc committee of concerned faculty. She had been asked to speak, from the perspective of someone who worked inside the State Department during the previous administration, on the failures of policy and diplomacy that led to the present crisis. I have allowed the poster announcing the event to be put up on the Northboro library bulletin board where I have been working part-time. I do not consider that I have exceeded my authority as public employee, cataloguer, or desk clerk by so doing.

I now sit here at my desk in the library and address

you directly: some careful speech for the pleasured man. I send you this and intend it as a pleasured system of direct address which, it is true, you haven't asked for, but which I consider, after much practice, useful for retaining in the memory certain events of family history. With this method I intend to make it possible for all three of us to hold events in memory so that we are able to speak directly concerning ourselves and others in the perfected pleasure of the burning air—something we were not able to do adequately that Thanksgiving afternoon on Hospital Hill. For now, I ask only that you consider the idea of some speech for another history.

As I hope you will quickly see, my method is simple and not at all demanding to learn. Its virtues—and difficulties, if any—will appear in the practice of the exercises, and in the development by each of you of the backgrounds and images needed to set in motion the practiced memory. But I am getting ahead of myself.

Let me present you with a summary of the method's five parts, so there will be no misleading suspense as to what I mean. There are five memory scenes of events in Lanham family history paired with five photographs—six, if you count the photograph from the State Department archives taken in China soon after the Boxer Rebellion. These pairings serve as backgrounds with which to hold the matter you wish to memorize in consciousness. My method shows you how to use these pairings to find your way, quickly and confidently, around and inside the memorized material, beginning anywhere and moving in any direction. There are five parts within each pairing of event and background, always in the same order, consisting of 1) some rule or sound of speech; 2) some short narrative of an event, often trivial, that involves a member of the Lanham family; 3) some piece of legal evidence, admissible in a court of international law, taken from first-hand testimony or Father's papers; 4) some principle or exercise designed to improve or strengthen memory technique, and 5) some sounded piece of direct address. Using these five divisions within each of the five pairings of memory scenes and photographs, I have found, is an efficient way both to hold in the mind and to develop the faculties necessary for a useful exercise of the rules of rhetoric. All commentators agree that the faculties involved are Invention, Arrangement, Style, and Delivery. Memory I treat as so important, intricate, delicate, and fragile a faculty that I have placed it carefully inside each pairing rather than, as most commentators do, treating it separately. So you see, my method consists really of only some one hundred moving parts. This number is well within the capacity of any young and flexible mind to master easily and should pose not the slightest difficulty for either of you.

Begin by committing to memory the five divisions of the five pairings and their order: again, these are, some rule of speech, some piece of family history, some direct evidence of Father's participation, between 7 February and 6 April 1965, in the planning and execution of war crimes—if he is not held legally accountable for his actions during this period, other indictments for criminal acts anyone might choose to bring against anyone else become travesties of reason and justice— some rule or exercise of applied mnemonics, and some fragment of direct address, delivered aloud as peroration in the pleasured air, suitable and fitting to the occasion.

Of course I am aware that you will have been encouraged to view me as someone afflicted with a

severe emotional and mental disorder, clinically documented and unsuccessfully treated, from which he has
self-evidently not fully been able to recover. I would
have you understand, and the exercises here are
designed to make that understanding useful, that the
method of direct address I am presenting to you is not
in the least incompatible with everyday functioning at
the highest levels. On the contrary, my experience has
been that my method, even when not being used to
organize a given occasion of speech, helps to lend clarity
to any matter at hand.

To illustrate, I reproduce here a letter I wrote to
my attorney. It relies upon my method without deriving
from it the full measure of coherence and the structures
of permanence which, I believe, give my method its
considerable value and make it deserving, I hope to
convince you, of both your time and respect. I trust you
will see from the letter's matter and style that my
method in no way interferes with the perfect execution
of everyday affairs, whether pertaining to matters of
greatest or least importance. Imagine some careful man
singing himself in this blue air; some German friend for
an idea of it afterwards.

Dear Elizabeth,

I very much appreciate the time you took with me last week, and your willingness to treat seriously what may have sounded like an odd request. Lawyers are no doubt trained by experience to keep straight faces in complicated family situations, but you seemed to have a genuine sympathy for what I'm trying to do for the children.

It was gratifying beyond what perhaps you quite appreciate that you did not treat my plans as simply the aberrant gesture of a not-fully-recovered psychiatric patient who, until recently, resided at the Conway Cooperative Care Center. That, of course, is the status I inescapably and rather publicly hold in a town this size, especially given the Lanham family's prominence and some of its members' past visibility in national political affairs.

Please go ahead and set things in motion to establish the trust according to the terms I indicated on Tuesday. You said the legalities would not be troublesome. Please have the eight hundred and fifty thousand dollars, plus the interest it accrues, divided equally between my nephew, Robert Lanham III (called "General" within the immediate family), now aged eleven (b. 6 April 1979) and Desmond Klare (b. 19 September 1980), aged ten, son of Lena Klare and Mathew Wright (divorced immediately after his birth, and, as far as I know, permanently estranged). Have the money entrusted to their absolute control and possession to be used for whatever purpose or purposes they wish on Des's twenty-first birthday.

Again, the only requirement of the trust should be that they accept possession of the pages of a letter to them that I will leave with you and which you and I have already discussed. There is nothing in the document intended to influence their decision concerning how they make use of the money.

As I told you, I hope still to be living in the Midwest when Des and General come into possession of the trust. Although I will supply you with my address, I leave it entirely up to them whether or not they wish to contact me, for whatever reason or reasons, once they have received my letter. I would ask only, should the occasion arise in the meantime—should my father or brother, for instance, legally question the purpose of my letter to the children (if such a thing is even feasible)

Invention

before the trust's provisions go into effect—that you, on my behalf, encourage the children not to dismiss out of hand the version of family history that I am passing on to them.

You are more than welcome to read the letter yourself when I forward it to you. How soon that will be I cannot now be certain. In the next few months I plan to pare and combine my several working drafts and then set the whole thing aside for some period—perhaps a considerable one. I will notify you of a date you can reasonably expect to receive it when I myself can better make an estimation. You will perhaps recognize the tone of voice in which I address the children from our meeting the other day, pitched a little differently, to be sure. What is missing now, and what I intend to place close to the beginning is a summary of relevant events. I realize that a common set of references for the years with which I am concerned are necessary to make myself understood, given all the time that will have elapsed. I want to emphasize that neither the outline I will provide nor the actual occurrence of the narrated events are in dispute. My narrative cannot, I assure you, be considered controversial or subject to refutation by any of the principals. In other words, there will be nothing in it pertaining to the family history that the children will not already have heard in one form or another from some family member or the adults around them. The actuality of the events is not the point, but rather its persistence, before and after Tet.

Thank you again for the time you took out of your busy schedule to meet with me on such short notice. I enjoyed our conversation very much.

Sincerely,

Garleth Lanham

In the art of remembering, the largest matters must be present along with the small. The various parts of speech and of your discourse will always lack their proper effect unless objects of different degrees and scale are held in mind simultaneously. Always use them together in pleasured speech. For instance, to hold the letter above in memory, be sure to go over it again in your mind's eye. Consider its matter, tone, style, purposes and its various orderings of words and phrases according to the five parts of rhetoric. It is the object, after all, of these pages to help you gain a certain mastery and a certain style of mastery. Again, the five faculties of rhetoric are, in their common ordering: Invention, Arrangement, Style, Memory, and Delivery. As I said, I have chosen to treat memory differently from other commentators, not because I value it less but, indeed, because I value it more.

Do not neglect to hold in mind, even when you are not engaged in formal speech, what rhetoric itself is: the task of discussing capably those things which law and custom have fixed for the uses of citizenship, and of securing, as far as possible, the agreement of your hearers.

Knowing the letters of the alphabet, you can inscribe on paper what is said in the pleasured air and can read aloud what you have written. In the same way, once you have learned the art of memory, you will be able to set in backgrounds what you have heard and from those backgrounds deliver it at any time in any order you choose or find it necessary to devise. Think of the backgrounds as the pages on which you write while the images you place within them are like the letters.

Consider the arrangement and disposition of the images as the script, and the delivery as the reading.

I will now describe for you the backgrounds and images that I have used and continue to use, not least in the composition of this letter. I can think of no better way of making my method available to you than to equip you with the backgrounds and images I myself have devised for speaking well so that you may practice with them yourselves. You need not rely on these—except in the very beginning—for your own progress. They are only exercises for you to practice with until you have developed a repertoire of backgrounds and images best suited to your own experience and pleasured histories. My backgrounds consist of the five photographs (four wire-service photos and a family snapshot) that were the only items pasted in an old scrapbook—like the ones you may remember Granny-Dad, Father's father, used to fill with pictures from hunting and fishing magazines— left with me by AG. He did so late one night in late May of 1978 on his way to a New Hampshire psychiatric hospital that specialized in long-term residential care. General, your father was on his way to admit himself to the private facility after failing to get the care he thought he needed from the doctors in Bethesda.

The images my method uses are from events of family history that I will now specify and narrate for you, since in only one of them were you yourselves active participants. The events are not what matter. They are done with. The point is to use them for your own progress in this art of pleasured speech. You should, of course, feel perfectly free to make them into things of your own, and I look forward with all my heart and mind to discovering someday what you will do with them. Just remember that the backgrounds and images the method uses are not meant to confine the free play of your minds or to hinder you in the development of backgrounds and images of your own.

Practice using the images and backgrounds my method proposes, remembering that they are meant to lead to satisfying occasions of direct speech and the pleasured will. I ask you to familiarize yourselves with the events and photographs laid out below. The method requires an easy familiarity with them before you begin to use them in the memorization and application of the method's numbered rules. Remember that our purpose, to state it slightly differently, is: some ordinary speech, along with adequate funds, for another history.

If you want to hold in memory a large number of things and make them available for speech (and I am assuming that you do), it is important to equip yourselves with a large number of backgrounds, so that in them you can set a large number of images. It is also necessary to place these backgrounds in a set series so that no confusion in their order can ever prevent you from following the images—that is, proceeding from any background you wish, whatever its place in the series in any direction—or from delivering in pleasured speech what has been committed to them.

I will now proceed to give you, by way of example, the backgrounds and images I have used to construct this method and an argument for why you should adopt it and make it your own. Again, for the five backgrounds I use the five photographs AG pasted in the old album that he left with me late one night in New Haven on his way to admit himself to a private psychiatric hospital in New Hampshire.

The first photograph is of a Buddhist monk, who has just emerged from the Embassy compound after a week of street violence and government repression. An agreement has been reached. He is in mid-stride, at a slight diagonal, crossing a wide, cobbled street. He is beginning to turn his head towards a jubilant, gesturing man, dressed in Western clothes, who is addressing the monk as if bringing him wondrous, important news together with greetings from friends with whom he had not expected to be reunited so soon.

The image from our family history I place within this background is of myself standing, screened by aspens recently planted next to the fairway on the new golf course bordering Father's Maryland house. It is an early sunlit morning in May of 1968, and I am looking towards the lawn of Father's house where Ellen, our mother's younger sister, stands holding a red gasoline can. From her stance I can tell that she is contemplating the act of pouring its contents over her white cotton dress and open, brown, lightly fringed leather jacket. I have been watching for some time and have not started to move towards her or call out.

The second background is a photograph of Father descending in Asia from the President's plane on 4 February 1965. He has been sent on short notice, at the personal request of the President, to obtain an accurate, first-hand view of the situation on the ground. Increasingly contradictory reports coming back to Washington from the Embassy, the intelligence community, and the military advisory mission have been contributing to an atmosphere of confusion and increasing alarm among the administration's top officials and chief foreign-policy planners.

The image I place there to hold in memory and illustrate my method's techniques is of AG, late one night sometime near the end of May 1978, standing in the doorway of my apartment in New Haven. Just beneath its usual, confident surface, his face looks both numbed and permanently startled in the low-watt glare of the hall light. He is handing me a battered photo album but refusing to come in. When I ask if I may accompany him wherever it is he is going, he shakes his head mildly with his casual, graceful air of command and assures me that I am not to worry, that he will be all right. He is just doing something that has to be done.

For the third background my method employs the obvious scene of the pleasured man burning in the middle of the city street. Having set himself on fire, he

---

burns as if he were saying something true. The wind wraps the flames around him and sends them out toward astonished onlookers quickly assembled.

The image my method places in this background is especially useful for illustrating the pleasures of memory—that pleasured speech attesting to the persistence of all the hapless, swarming dead for whom we are, after all, responsible. It is of Lena suddenly standing up during a planning meeting at Ernie Glauber's ranch in New Mexico in March of 1983. She and I were both part of the consulting team assigned to help Glauber, a retired army colonel, create a documentary film—we were there to draft an outline and preliminary shooting script—sponsored by the public-affairs office of the State Department. It was to be used by American foreign-aid personnel throughout Latin America. Its purpose was to explain and promote the administration's Development for Democracy Program to high government officials and their staffs. Its stated goal was to enlist the business interests in such countries, especially in Central America, in support of electoral reform. The argument we were to offer was that open, professionally run, fair elections were the only way to ensure the allegiance of an emerging stratum of middle-class professionals and white-collar service workers in those economically developing societies and so of assuring long-term social stability and economic growth for the region as a whole. Do not be surprised, reading this, at my participation in such an effort. I was then, after all, far from developing or practicing any discipline of memory such as this one.

To use this image, it is only important to note here that Lena is reacting to a slide Ernie Glauber has just projected on the screen. He is gesturing towards a sepia photograph fixing the light of the blade's blurred descent at a public beheading of a petty thief in Peiping, China in 1904. He is trying to convince us that this would be an ideal way to illustrate the proposition that the social rancors bred by the brutality sometimes tolerated under autocratic, traditionalist regimes ultimately have a negative impact on economic modernization. They hinder, he explains, the institutional development necessary for social stability in the midst of dynamic capitalist expansion oriented to a newly emerging global marketplace. Lena is suddenly standing and speaking. Her soft voice sounds like ice glazing a round stone. She is saying, "No. For you, any brown girl will do." In the quiet afterwards her eyes seem to take us in as if from a great distance. The room feels newly made. She sits down again. We decide not to use the photograph.

This image is as clear to me as all the others, and I continue to use it to hold in consciousness and explicate events of family history. Nevertheless, I should advise you that Lena, when I recalled the incident to her, remembered no such moment and no such speech. I cannot pretend to explain it. I offer it for your use and trust that you will not find it discreditable to me or to my method's reliability.

As the fourth background my method uses a scene of dense smoke rising from behind a nondescript stone located on top of a low hill, identified as a Buddhist shrine in an accompanying caption. The smoke is from Cholon, the Chinese section of the city, which is burning just below. A helicopter hovers above.

The image I have chosen to place here for safekeeping is of myself grabbing and briefly holding the white softness of the front of Father's shirt. As usual, he is not wearing his suitcoat. I am leaning across his wide desk, and he reaches to press a button somewhere underneath, alerting security. I am suddenly motionless, held by hands that come out of nowhere in a position that feels effortlessly calm, past some natural barrier of brutality, having arrived at this choreographed breaking point without foreknowledge or practical preparation. You will have heard of this incident as the time I tried to assault my father while he was at work in his office. It came up repeatedly in the judge's chambers and figures prominently in the court papers we signed.

For the fifth background my method uses the picture that formally caused all the trouble in the family. It shows AG as a second lieutenant standing with six of his men beside a pile of dead bodies that are stacked with military precision. One kneeling soldier, posing in front and a little to the left, is smiling with a gleeful, boyish happiness. He holds something up to the camera. Looking closely, you can tell that it is a necklace of ears. This is the photograph I would not give back, either to AG or Father. Both they and other immediate family members, continue to insist that no such photograph ever existed.

The image my method places in this background, and which I use here for illustrative purposes—also, of

course, as a way of storing it in memory's safekeeping—
is of the three of us on Hospital Hill flying kites two
Thanksgiving afternoons ago. We are watching Father,
AG, Lena and two policemen approach us from the road
below. They are approaching with the intent of taking
me into custody, possessing, as they do, an order for
your protection, alleging that I am actively jeopardizing
your welfare as minors by being in your company. You
are aged eight and nine.

The object of reading this should be to invent some
public speech with which to make the presence of the
dead visible: some other history, some practical method
by which to be able to speak capably concerning those
things which law and custom have assigned to the uses
of citizenship and to secure, as far as it is possible to do
so, the agreement of your listeners.

These then are the five backgrounds with sample
images stored in them my method of direct address
uses to explain itself and demonstrate its usefulness. I
urge you to adopt these as your own and use them until
you have had a chance to develop others that you may
find more suitable to your present occasion.

Hold now in your minds the task of rhetoric which is to discuss capably those things that law and custom have assigned to the duties of citizenship, and to secure, as far as it is possible, the agreement of your hearers.

Go over in your minds and hold in your memories the five parts of rhetoric without which some direct speech for another history will not be possible: invention, arrangement, style, memory, and delivery.

Establish in your memories, and renew them often by calling them to mind, the five backgrounds—and their images—from which this method is constructed. Keep, if useful, the names I have given them, realizing that close acquaintance permits the friendliness and informality of nominative variation: the happy man upon his unexpected release, Father descending in Asia, the pleasured man burning, smoke rising from Cholon, and AG's necklace.

Go over the five parts and their names into which, in their turn, each pairing of background and image is divided. It is through these divisions that the pairings can be made to release the rich storehouse of materials they are holding. Again, the five parts and their names are: some rule or sound of speech, some event of family history, some admissible piece of evidence—in a court of international law or before a duly constituted war-crimes tribunal of recognized legal standing—some technique of memory, some local instance of direct address.

Having committed to memory the parts of the method presented so far and having made sure through practice that they are available easily according to the motions of your pleasured wills, you are ready to proceed. The introductory material is now concluded. From here the method unfolds systematically until it reaches its end.

Now, however, I find myself on the verge of the usual mistake. It is two-fold. First, in an effort to avoid prolixity, I have neglected to stress enough this important injunction: theory without continuous practice in speaking is of little avail; from this you may understand that the precepts of theory here offered ought to be applied in practice. Second, I have not taken sufficient care to acquaint you with the difference this method makes in the speech of its user in this pleasured air. I am in danger of taking for granted what, in fact, should be made plain when introducing any new thing to others: that the true quality of the state of that thing's lack can only be appreciated through its mastery. To illustrate this latter point, I reproduce now the very first draft of this letter, written to you before I myself had mastered the exercises of my own design. Although I realize that this means a slight delay in your acquisition of the method itself, I include it here to illustrate the mistakes in speaking all of us are prone to when we do not attend to, and train ourselves in, the parts of rhetoric in their proper order. From what I have said already, you will recognize the general sense of what it is I want to say to you in what follows, but will readily perceive the absence of my own mastery or accomplished use of my own method.

Dear General and Des,

Some idea of her burning; this pleasure of rule: five scenes for memory, five photographs for backgrounds, five images to place there for a method with which to present it in a pleasured style. Invention, of course, is the devising of matter, true or plausible, that would make the case convincing. Hold in the mind some pleasant view and rehearse the matter to be recited inwardly. The President, he said, has approved a change of mission to permit the troops' more active use. Father signed the memorandum in the President's name. We believe, he said, that the best available way of increasing our chance of success is the development and execution of a policy of *sustained reprisal*—a policy justified by the whole campaign of violence and terror in the south. Measured against the costs of defeat, this program seems cheap. And even if it fails to turn the tide—as it may—the value of the effort seems to us to exceed its cost. We need to conduct the application of force so that there is always the prospect of worse to come.

Memory is the faculty of clearly discerning and remembering our ideas, and of calling to mind the fittest words by which to express them. We should, he said, develop and exercise the option to retaliate against *any* act of violence to persons or property.

Delivery is the faculty of the right and just management of voice, look, and gesture. Do not look indifferent. Just enunciation is a kind of commentary. You should therefore always be sure not to read anything in public without having carefully read it over to yourselves in private. The political values of reprisal, he said, require a *continuous* operation. The italics are in the original document.

Practice some method of direct address with which to produce sound in the pleasured mouth for another history.

You will have to say it yourself eventually in the perfect, ordinary air: some speech to hold the pleasured voice, this bright air, the virtue of his will. Any accurate family history must include him saying we should execute our reprisal policy with as low a level of public noise as possible. It is to our interest that our acts should be seen—but we do not wish to boast about them in ways that make it hard to shift ground.

Again: some sound for it in the pleasured mouth, some German friend for an idea of it afterwards, some French relief for a failure of nerve, some idea of her burning: this caroling man singing of empire. We should conduct the application of force so that there is always the prospect of worse to come.

Sincerely,

As you make yourselves acquainted with my method,

both in theory and practice, you will see that the letter above possesses the right tone and is not at fault in its words, but fails to secure the agreement of listeners. It lacks, above all else, a practiced idea of the ordered act and what task is to be accomplished by persuasion.

Some sound of speech in the pleasured mouth for another history: There are three kinds of causes which a speaker must treat: epideictic, deliberative, and judicial. The epideictic is devoted to praise or censure of a particular person. The deliberative consists of the discussion of policy and embraces persuasion and dissuasion. The judicial concerns legal controversy and consists of the conduct of civil suits or criminal prosecution and defense.

We almost never saw Father during that time between 1963 and the late spring of 1965 when he was busy developing and persuading the bureaucracy to execute administration policy. It was he who provided the line of argument the government would use to defend the war internally as well as publicly. That he and our mother's sister Ellen were lovers—and had been since before the wedding—was accepted by everyone, including, as I understand it, the sisters, with the stipulation that it was never, in the perfected sense of that word, to be mentioned. The unmistakable advantages of the way Anna Bascomb's marriage to Richard Lanham consolidated and renewed family alliances of several generations' duration were appreciated, gently and smilingly, and then passed over by everyone. As a family, we inhabited a time to which, it was assumed, we had inherited the right through natural superiority, whose exemptions we were both to master and to find, or marry, the means to afford. It was the nature of Ellen's personal involvement under the circumstances that lent her act of protest concerning the war its tainted and compromised aura within the family. In the actual event, I watched Father, dressed in his old blue bathrobe, running across the lawn in the spring light holding, in front of him in both hands, the carriage blanket from the study. Ellen was suddenly holding, as if at the greatest possible distance from her body, a match whose tiny flame leapt in the strong spring light. When Father reached her, he wrapped her and rolled with her in the new light across the wet grass. He called an ambulance and Ellen was hospitalized. The local paper carried the story of an early morning medical emergency involving a guest staying at the Presidential Special Assistant's Maryland home, but none of the national papers picked it up. I stood in that stand of trees watching from the edge of the golf course for the rest of that day. This is the scene I saw for years—and from which I tried to protect you when in your company.

It was Father who wrote and signed what you must practice hearing as evidence properly admissible in an international court of law: We believe that the best available way of increasing our chance of success is the development and execution of a policy of *sustained reprisal*. We should develop and exercise the option to retaliate against *any* act of violence to persons or property. Measured against the costs of defeat, this program seems cheap. And even if it fails to turn the tide—as it may—the value of the effort seems to us to exceed its cost.

I refused to serve in the armed forces of our country and was granted the legal status of conscientious objector by Northboro's selective-service board on the grounds that I had applied at the time of my registration, and not at the time I was ordered to report for induction. The statutory guidelines, I believe, expressly declared those to be insufficient grounds for granting my classification. This local policy guideline was, however, instituted suddenly by the discretionary authority of the chairman of the local draft board three days before the scheduled hearing of my case. Although it was never spoken of within the family or among close family friends, there was much obvious embarrassment surrounding my case, given Father's role in the administration. People, in indirect ways, expressed their sympathy for Father's awkward and delicate position. Among themselves, but sometimes within his hearing and mine, they also indicated how impressed they were by the honesty, straightforwardness, and resigned stoicism with which he handled the situation, both in public and within the immediate family.

My case was decided without a hearing, though I can't now remember how I was informed of its outcome. I think a phone call came notifying me of a postponement and then a letter simply arrived cancelling the hearing and issuing my reclassification. Of course, AG, as the older brother, did what was expected of him, and much more.

You must understand, and respect accordingly, the

fact that, of the five faculties necessary for pleasured speech, memory is the treasure house of the ideas supplied by invention and the guardian of all the parts of rhetoric. Some careful men designate it a separate part of rhetoric, but I hold it to be so important that I have given it its own place and number—four—within each serial treatment of the pairings of a scene from family history and a photograph. The art of memory is the firm retention in the mind of the matter, words, and arrangement of what is to be said.

Recite from memory, now and as often as is necessary, the five faculties necessary to the art of rhetoric, the three types of causes that rhetoric treats, and the five backgrounds my own method uses. Again, they are: the happy man upon his sudden release; Father descending in Asia; the pleasured man burning; smoke rising from Cholon; AG and his men—one of whom is holding a necklace of ears. Give the definition best suited to describe the faculty of memory and place firmly there, using images and backgrounds, the reasons Father gave for the policy he invented and the executive order implementing it which he signed in the President's name.

Compose some direct speech for an idea of the careful man singing himself home—some sweet invective in this blue air; some time of speech, some idea of it afterwards: Catullus in exile, sympathetic to empire, asking, Was it for this that you went to open up the western lands? Was it for this that you disturbed the world and created ruin? Don't be afraid that he won't understand. At Yale, Father majored in both classics and math.

Use invention for the six parts of discourse which consist of, in their proper order, the introduction, the statement of facts, division, proof, refutation, and conclusion. Remember that all the faculties having to do with rhetoric can be acquired by three means: theory, imitation, and practice. You must know the nature of the cause you will be arguing in order to determine the character of the introduction and the other parts to employ. There are four kinds of causes: the honorable, the discreditable, the doubtful, and the petty. The introduction, depending upon the nature of the cause, should employ either the direct opening or the subtle approach in order to win the favorable attention of your hearers. The statement of facts or narration can take one of three forms: legendary, historical, or realistic. The legendary comprises events neither true nor probable, like those narratives used by tragedy. The historical is an account of exploits actually performed but removed in time from the recollection of our own age. Realistic narrative recounts imaginary events which could have occurred, as in the plots of comedies. The statement of facts should have three qualities: brevity, clarity, and plausibility. You need to learn how to achieve all of these qualities. Fabrication must be circumspect in those matters in which official documents or some person's unimpeachable guarantee can or will be proved to have played a role.

Although I tried, I could not get AG to stay the night that he appeared and handed me the album with the five photographs pasted inside. I could not think of anything to say that would make him stay.

Some speech for the pleasured man; some idea of him singing.

I sensed that he was both excited and relieved to be doing what he had finally made up his mind to do. Of course, he was defying Father by going back to the doctor and the hospital from which Father had removed him in 1970. (He had first checked himself in there when he had needed help so badly after his tour of duty.) But I don't think AG saw it as defiance. Maybe he felt he needed to test himself again by jeopardizing his promising new Defense Department job analyzing the policy implications of recent arms-control proposals. He had called me just a few weeks before to tell me how excited he was by the intellectual challenge and the prospect of having a real role in formulating our government's negotiating position. Now it was as if he were back on long-range reconnaissance patrol, had reconnoitred to the edge of being a good son, and was about to break into open country. Underneath, I sensed that he was quite agitated. I did not want him to drive anywhere that night. And I certainly did not want him to be alone.

All AG actually said to me was "Keep these," as he handed me the album. Maybe he needed to know that I had those particular photographs in my possession in order to do whatever it was he was going to discover he wanted to or had to do. As it turned out, of course, Father used his considerable influence and managed in less than forty-eight hours to have him discharged from the New Hampshire facility. Father himself accompanied him back to Maryland aboard a private plane, and signed the papers placing him under the care of military doctors at Bethesda. I learned all this much later. At the time, I believed AG when he told me that he had changed his mind after realizing the implications for his career and his family. Or I told myself that I did. I don't know the truth of this now.

At any rate, it was not until I was working on the Development for Democracy project in March of 1983 that I learned how adamant Father was that AG recover the album. Father had evidently first learned of my having it on the plane trip back to Maryland in 1978, but had decided not to do anything about it then. AG called me while I was in New Mexico and told me that Father would use every means at his disposal to obtain the photographs from me if I didn't return them immediately to either AG or himself without copying them. The urgency, I think, came from the fact that AG's name was beginning to be mentioned for sensitive positions both at Defense and State. These would, of course, involve rigorous background checks, perhaps even closed-session Congressional confirmation hearings. When I told AG that I had no intention of returning the photographs but that I also had no intention of ever showing them to anyone, he turned into his own version of Father. He threatened all kinds of things, starting with barring access to you, General, who were all of four at the time. He assured me that the rest of the family backed him up on this. Force, both physical and legal, was clearly implied. I again explicitly refused to return the album to him or to Father. He issued me his personal ultimatum and demanded them in the name of responsibility to the family and, in particular, in the name of his responsibility to you as his son.

I held onto the photographs because I knew Father and AG would destroy them—not because I had any plans to use them. Even then, however, I think I obscurely sensed that I wanted to preserve them somehow as private aids in the proper cultivation of a disciplined memory. It turned out that the lawyers even found a way to make the ultimate disposition of the photographs—without specifying their subject matter—a formal part of the legal agreement under whose terms I am writing you this letter and transferring into your hands my part of the Lanham estate. Elizabeth did not think we should object, saying that, in practice, the provision, as written, was unenforceable and reminding me that, according to what I had told her, the photographs were, in any case, unrecoverable.

Article Six of the constitution of the International Military Tribunal states: The following acts, or any of them, are crimes coming within the jurisdiction of the Tribunal for which there shall be individual responsibility: a) Crimes against peace: namely, planning, preparation, initiation, or waging of a war of aggression or participation in a common plan or conspiracy for the accomplishment of such a war; b) War crimes: namely, the wanton destruction of cities, towns or villages, or devastation not justified by military necessity; c) Crimes against humanity: namely, murder and other inhumane acts committed against any civilian population, before or during the war. Leaders, organizers, instigators and accomplices participating in the formulation or execution of a common plan or conspiracy to commit any of the foregoing crimes are responsible for all acts performed by any persons in execution of such plans. Article Seven states: The official position of defendants, whether as Heads of State or responsible officials in Government Departments, shall not be considered as freeing them from responsibility or mitigating punishment. And Article Eight states: The fact that the defendant acted pursuant to order of his Government or of a superior shall not free him from responsibility, but may be considered in mitigation of punishment if the Tribunal determines that justice so requires.

Remember always to include in its proper place, using the appropriate words and memorable images, some speech for the idea of Father writing, for the President's action, we are convinced that the political values of reprisal require a *continuous* operation. The great merit of the proposed scheme is that to stop it they would have to stop enough of their activity to permit the probable success of a determined pacification effort. At the same time it should be recognized that, in order to maintain the power of reprisal without risk of excessive loss, an air war may in fact be necessary.

Some pleasured speech for an idea of it in the burning air.

There are no tricks of memory, only techniques— and the obligation to connect them to the pleasured will. If we do not wish to use the direct opening, we must begin our speech with a law, a written document, or some argument supporting our cause. We can make our hearers well disposed towards what we say by four methods: by discussing ourselves, by discussing our adversaries, by discussing our hearers directly, or by discussing the facts.

There are two kinds of memory, the natural and the artificial. The natural memory is that memory which is embedded in our minds and is born simultaneously with thought. The artificial memory is that memory which is developed and strengthened by a kind of training and by discipline. The two kinds reinforce and help each other in all things, but neither should be relied upon alone in the education of the pleasured will.

Practice some speech for the idea of the caroling man singing of empire in a direct and pleasured style. Practice, with fresh words, backgrounds, and images, this sound—holding in the mind, both for pleasure and understanding, its perfect, sursum corda of timbre, pitch, and rhythm: I do not care to concern / my pleasured self / with whether / Caesar's skin is dark or fair. / The object, surely, is to be / just: citizen and son.

I have begun to discuss and you have begun to practice the art of rhetoric mostly with respect to its judicial aspect. Do not forget that rhetoric also includes the epideictic and the deliberative. Deliberative speech concerns a choice between two courses of action, or the choice of one course among many that are being considered. An example of a choice between two courses of action is the question: Is it better to destroy Carthage or leave her standing? An example of a choice among many is the question: When empire becomes the last resort of free men, what voice should be used by those whose task it is to teach children justice? The object in deliberative speech is always to obtain advantage which, in turn, has two aspects: security and honor. Security also can be divided into two aspects: might and craft. Might is determined by armies, fleets, arms, engines of war, the recruiting of men, and other similar things. Craft is exercised by money, promises, dissimulation, surprise, deception and other similar means. All of these are topics you may wish to take up for yourselves at another time, depending upon your needs and purposes. Honor can be divided into that which is right and that which is praiseworthy. The right is that which is in accordance with virtue and duty. The right can be considered under the headings of wisdom, justice, courage, and temperance. Wisdom is intelligence that, with training, is able to distinguish between good and bad. The knowledge of an art is also to be considered as wisdom, and, of course, a well-furnished memory, or experience in many things, is to be considered wisdom as well. Justice is equity, giving to each thing what it is due in equal proportion to its worth. Courage is reaching for great things and having contempt for that which is mean; also enduring hardship for the sake of what it is you are after. Temperance is the discipline of will to restrain desire. The praiseworthy is what produces an honorable remembrance at the time of the event and afterwards.

Some German friend for an idea of it. I went to Ernie Glauber's ranch in the hills of the Sangre de Cristo Mountains in New Mexico in late March of 1983 as an employee of Petrie Associates, a consulting firm. The company had been awarded a contract by an inter-agency government task force to come up with a two-year implementation plan and a six-week demonstra-tion pilot project for the administration's Development for Democracy Program. Of course, I got the job due to Father, who had known Petrie since Groton and worked with him often on special projects needing both specialized empirical research and sensitive political handling. To myself, I justified accepting Petrie's offer because he claimed he was approaching me on his own initiative, having read a paper I published while still in graduate school on the ways the symbolization process, fostered and preserved within traditional Iroquois mourning ceremonies, had strengthened resistance to modernization.

Des, I did not know your mother was going to be working on the project until we found ourselves together at the airport waiting for the same flight to Albuquerque. She had been a student of Father's when he taught a post-doctoral seminar in international law and foreign policy at Georgetown in 1979—and soon became much more than that, of course, staying at the Maryland house most of that next year while both pregnant with you and separating from your father. During the week, Father usually stayed at his mother's townhouse in Georgetown when he was in Washington. I was in the Yale graduate program in anthropology then but visited the Maryland house for an extended period that summer. Not surprisingly, Lena went on to work at the State Department where she helped draft policy initiatives on both the Middle East peace process and aid programs for East Africa. She left the government in 1989 when, with Father's help, she was offered a job teaching political science at Salisbury College, where, of course, Anna also taught in the English and Composition Department, having found a job there in the mid-70s after she and Father were divorced. I am always struck by how close Father liked to keep all of us—even as he was emphasizing the strenuously impersonal imperatives of service and stewardship. Duty, he liked to say, was a sovereign country without borders.

When I saw Lena in the airport, I suddenly felt happy and even grateful for no reason that was immediately obvious to me. I suggested that we have our seat assignments changed so that we could sit together on the plane. She agreed. There was no difficulty arranging this, and we talked easily for the next four hours. Des, this is when I first heard about you and your delighted happiness in collecting bright stones and making things. You were only two and a half, and Lena said you could not be made to understand why you couldn't help her do her work so she wouldn't have to go so far away. You were a frighteningly precocious child which is why I never worried when there was all that concern later over your supposed difficulties learning to read.

On the plane, Lena told me that she was representing the position of those in the State Department who wanted to focus American policy on encouraging business elites within Latin American countries to put serious pressure on their militaries to back electoral reforms. We could sell this position domestically, she assured me, because it was a step toward securing long-term social stability and predictable market conditions throughout the region. Our job, she thought, was to convince influential junior officers within those militaries that their own futures depended upon the confidence of the international business community for whom gradual but real political reform was a necessity. In return, she argued, our government should continue to guarantee substantial loan packages to the military governments for long-term economic development projects as well as direct military and economic assistance over the next several years. The obvious problem for us would be how to offer meaningful policy recommendations without addressing the specific conditions of each country individually. We discussed the possibility of suggesting to Glauber that he include country-specific participants in the project who might critique our plans before their final implementation with respect to any particular government. The documentary film whose development and production Petrie Associates was to oversee would be designed for carefully screened groups of businessmen and women and for reform-minded government and military personnel as part of a general Development for Democracy policy initiative to be coordinated through American embassies and consulates throughout Latin America. To this day, I do not know how much, if any, of this project was ever put into practice. Never having heard anything more of it, I strongly suspect that it was dropped at the time of the Hassenfus mess in the fall of 1986 and the subsequent Congressional outrage over the disclosures of our government's Central American policies.

Nevertheless, I took immeasurable pleasure in speaking with Lena on that plane trip, high in the cold brightness of that blue air. I have been trying to find a way to speak of it ever since—to give you some idea of it afterwards.

Practice holding in the mind, using the backgrounds and images you have chosen, the idea of what Father actually said. He wrote on a yellow legal pad while on board the President's plane flying home from Asia. He was charged with bringing back a plan on which the President and nation could act: We want to keep before the enemy the carrot of our desisting as well as the stick of continued pressure. We also need to conduct the application of force so that there is always the prospect of worse to come. We cannot assert that a policy of sustained reprisal will succeed in changing the course of the contest. It may fail, and we cannot estimate the odds of success with any accuracy—they may be somewhere between 25% and 75%. What we can say is that, even if it fails, the policy will be worth it. At a minimum it will damp down the charge that we did not do all that we could have done, and this charge will be important in many countries, including our own. Beyond that, a reprisal policy—to the extent it demonstrates U.S. willingness to employ this new norm in counter-insurgency—will set a higher price for the future upon all adventures of guerrilla warfare, and it should therefore somewhat increase our ability to deter such adventures. We must recognize, however, that that ability will be severely weakened if there is failure for any reason.

Commit some pleasured speech to memory for the sound of empire: We need to study with special care the backgrounds we have adopted so that they may cling lastingly in our memory, for the images, like letters, are effaced when we make no use of them. The backgrounds, like wax tablets, should abide. And that we may by no chance err in the number of backgrounds, each fifth background should be specially marked. For example, if in the fifth we set a golden hand, and in the tenth some acquaintance whose first name is Decimus, it will then be easy to place similar markers in each successive fifth background.

In some careful, pleasured tone, practice the art of direct address, taking full advantage of the vocative. Above all, do not be embarrassed or reluctant to use it for your own enjoyment: Degenerate Caesar, how can you stand watching it? / After Spain was so recently stripped, / now Gaul / and next Britain will feel / a nervous shiver. / You will make us make you into a god / But I prefer this idea of myself: / Some careful man singing himself home / in this blue and pleasured air.

When considering how to speak of Father's pleasured acts of state, or the acts of any other person, it is necessary to examine whether they are in accordance with the law. Once again, we are speaking with regard to the judicial part of rhetoric. We can discuss this topic capably only when we know the departments by which the law is constituted. These departments are as follows: nature, statute, custom, previous judgments on the same kind of cause, equity, and agreement. To the law of nature belong the duties of kinship and family loyalty. According to this kind of law parents are cherished by their children, and children by their parents. Statute law is that law which is sanctioned by the will of the people. For instance, when summoned one must appear before the court. There are no exemptions from this rule. Legal custom is that which, absent any statute, is endowed by usage with the force of statute law. It is understood, for example, that money you have deposited with a banker is recoverable from his partner. A previous judgment obtains when, on the same question, a sentence has been passed or a decree issued. These can vary greatly; different decisions will have been reached by different judges or officials. The law rests on equity when it seems to agree with truth and the general welfare. Sometimes, according to circumstance and a person's status, a new kind of law may well be established. It is law founded on agreement if the parties have drawn up a contract or covenant between them. These then are the divisions of the law by which one should establish the justice or injustice of an act. Without an applied art of rhetoric, this task cannot be done, which is why I have been at some pains to supply you with a reliable means of acquiring, for yourselves and for your own purposes, a useable method of direct address.

It is not hard to devise matter to support a cause, but to polish what has been devised and to give it an easy, natural delivery is often very difficult. Only the possession of a method such as this will keep you from dwelling longer than necessary on the same topics, returning again and again to the same place, abandoning an argument or chain of reasoning before it has been completed, or making an inappropriate transition to the next one. By following this method, you insure that your hearers will perceive and remember the distribution of the parts of your speech as a whole as well as following each of its arguments to its conclusion.

Remember that it is important to go over the backgrounds often. Be sure to practice using them at least once a day, no matter how busy you are or how pressing the day's other events may seem.

It was only after I learned that Father had dissuaded AG from his announced decision to leave the Defense Department and pursue the dream of making his own life that I finally dared address him directly concerning his acts regarding his eldest son. I found out that last evening in New Mexico from an inadvertent reference AG made in the same phone call in which he threatened me with a perfect and limitless harm. He had been drinking for a day and a half, he said, when I asked him. He knew me well enough, he said, to know that I would use those photographs someday against everyone and everything he loved. I had only refused to give Father my word as his son that I would destroy them.

The next day, before I left Glauber's ranch, I called

Father in Washington and demanded to see him. He reluctantly agreed to see me in his office late the following afternoon but warned me that, as matters stood, he saw nothing to discuss. He cited my previous refusal to surrender the photographs and what he considered my unconscionable irresponsibility to my brother and endangerment of the whole family. He accused me of exploiting my brother's temporary emotional distress in the service of my own self-aggrandizing and unconfronted Oedipal aggressions. He could not allow my psychological problems, he said, to harm the entire family. I nonetheless insisted on seeing him and said he could expect me the next day, with or without an appointment.

You must understand that I did not know what I wanted to say to him. This was, of course, before I had begun to develop and practice the pleasured method of direct address that I am offering you here. All I knew was that I needed to hear the sound of his voice to picture what it was he thought he was doing. I could not remember ever having heard him speak as if, legally, someone had the right to question him directly concerning anything he said or did. I recalled AG telling me of a sudden vision he had had once while there. He mockingly called it an anti-epiphany. Pinned down by sniper fire from a hamlet he and his men had just searched without result, he suddenly saw, he told me, in a voice that seemed both stunned and resigned, the true pleasure of being Father's son. It was the sensation of sleeping inside an open eye watching the world as it burned and registering, without feeling, the ecstasy of its absolute beauty.

I wanted Father to have to say something about AG, and I would answer. Some pleasured speech for another history.

Hold in mind with backgrounds and images, so that you can repeat the words themselves, some idea of Father inscribing, on yellow legal paper aboard the President's plane, the following: In partnership with the government of our ally, we should develop and exercise the option to retaliate against *any* act of violence to persons or property. In practice, we may wish at the outset to relate our reprisals to those acts of relatively high visibility such as the recent incident at the airfield. Later, we might retaliate against the assassination of a province chief, but not necessarily the murder of a hamlet official; we might retaliate against a grenade thrown into a crowded café in the capital, but not necessarily to a shot fired into a small shop in the countryside. We should announce that our two governments have been patient and forbearing in the hope that the opposition would come to its senses without the necessity of our having to take further action; but the outrages continue and now we must react against those who are responsible; we will not provoke; we will not use our force indiscriminately; but we can no longer sit by in the face of repeated acts of terror and violence for which the enemy is responsible. The essence of our explanation should be that our actions are intended solely to insure the effectiveness of a policy of reprisal, and in no sense represent any intent to wage offensive war. These distinctions should not be difficult to develop.

Hold in the mind some speech for the sound of Father singing in this bright air. It is advantageous to obtain backgrounds in a deserted rather than a populous region, because the passing to and fro of people confuse and weaken the impression of the images, while solitude keeps their outlines sharply defined. Also, be careful to secure backgrounds of different kinds using different forms of architecture so that each may be kept distinct in the memory. For example, if you choose many places set among columns, however strongly you may differentiate the columns themselves, you will not be able to keep track of which spaces you placed which images in. The backgrounds ought to be of moderate size—too big and the images become vague, too small and they will be squeezed without sufficient room to accommodate orderly arrangement. The backgrounds should be neither too bright nor too dim, so that shadows neither obscure the images nor brightness make them glitter and so blur their shapes. The intervals between backgrounds should be suitably spaced, about thirty feet some commentators have said, for like the external eye, the inner eye of thought is less powerful when you have moved the object of attention too near or too far away.

This method is designed to enable you to say suddenly what is necessary, if the situation demands it: some sweet invective for the pleasured man. It is designed also to help you invent some careful speech for the caroling man afterwards: For the sake of this bastard's pleasured gain, Father, / you broke the back of the world / losing everything? First he ripped / his own patrimony to pieces, / next he took Pontus / then Spain.

Practice some pleasured rule for an idea of them approaching us on Hospital Hill. Learn some pleasured method of speech as an aid to memory. In deliberation, the object is to achieve through argument a course of action from among one or several others being considered or advised. In epideictic speech, the object is to praise or censure. The following topics are available for use in this kind of speech: external circumstances, physical attributes, and qualities of character. External circumstances are the result of fortune, favorable or adverse, and are as follows: descent, education, wealth, power, occasions of fame, citizenship, friendship, and their contraries. Physical attributes are merits or defects of the body produced by nature such as agility, strength, beauty, health, and their contraries. Qualities of character rest upon judgment and thought. These consist of wisdom, justice, courage, temperance, and their contraries. These will make up the matter to be used in the proof and refutation. The division will be as follows: we shall set forth the things we intend to praise or censure; then recount the events, observing their precise sequence and chronology, so that one may understand what the person under discussion did, and with what prudence or caution. But it will first be necessary to set forth his virtues or faults of character, and then to explain how, such being his character, he has used the advantages or disadvantages of his physical or of his external circumstances. The following is the order we must keep when portraying a life: external circumstances, physical advantages, character. What has been his attitude in the exercise of his prerogatives? If he is dead, what sort of death did he die, and what consequences followed upon it? This mode of address should not be neglected just because it is seldom employed by itself, independently of other matters, occasions, and purposes.

I have now completed treating the hardest part of my method which is invention and its application to the three divisions of rhetorical occasion, and I will now proceed to the topic of arrangement. In the background you will be using for this part of the method: AG is standing all the way to the right of his men. The smiling soldier is kneeling in front to the left, holding a necklace of ears up to the camera. In demanding that I return this photograph, Father said it could only mis-

lead anyone who saw it. I tell you this now because it is
important for you to understand that he is right. This
was the photograph that Father didn't want you to see.
He was convinced that I would show it to you that late
Thanksgiving afternoon on Hospital Hill which is why
he, AG, Lena and the two police officers were approaching us from the bottom of the hill while we were flying
the kite. Once you decided on a course of action, Father
used to say, there was no point in not going to the limit
to execute it. There was never any excuse, he said, not
to fight the good fight. He had taken AG and Lena with
him and had managed to have them convince a judge to
swear out, on your behalves, an order of protection
against me, alleging that I had lured you away from
Anna's house and was actively endangering your welfare by having you in my presence. Needless to say, I
was easily able to refute such accusations with Elizabeth acting as my attorney and the testimony of various
friends and former colleagues—not to mention my psychological evaluation tests, which were officially made
a part of the court record. But that, of course, was not
until after I had been taken into preventative custody
in front of you.

Do you remember that faded little red and yellow mesh bag I showed you while we were getting the kite ready to fly? I asked each of you to put something in it that the kite could take away with it. General, you put in a white pebble from the ground and a dime from your pocket, asking me if I could promise that it would not fall out. Des, you finally decided to put in a shoelace from your sneaker when I reminded you of the running man you wanted me to explain in the background of that painting by Uccello we found looking at a book together in the library. Remember when I told you laughing that he was the kind of soldier I wanted to be, someone running from the scene, pretending to be helping a wounded man or bringing news? You protested that I couldn't be someone in a painting. That was when I realized I could write to you in this way.

I assume that each of you has your own memories of that Thanksgiving afternoon, so I do not need to present the scene again here. As you may have guessed, the small packet, wrapped in the dark blue cloth, that was already in the mesh bag when you put in the things you chose in our game, held the photographs AG had given me to keep for him. I had removed them from the album that morning. I wanted some way to make you aware of them before they disappeared. Father was right about that.

Some pleasured speech for empire and democracy. It is a classic mistake to try to have them both, but we always do. Father already knew, when he ordered it, that the bombing would not prevent the internal collapse of the government we said we were saving. Develop carefully the images and backgrounds to hold in your minds Father's actual speech in the burning air: It remains quite possible, however, that this reprisal policy would get us quickly into the level of military activity contemplated in the so-called Phase II of our planning. It may even get us beyond this level with both the neighboring foreign governments if there is enemy counter-action. We and our allies should be prepared for a level of armed violence, especially in urban areas, that would dwarf anything yet experienced. These a re the risks of any action. They should be carefully reviewed—but we believe them to be acceptable. We are convinced that the political values of reprisal require a *continuous* operation. Episodic responses would lack the persuasive force of sustained pressure.

Some pleasured speech for an idea of it afterwards; some German friend for an idea of it spoken in this bright and present air.

Some pleasured speech for an idea of memory; some careful way of saying it. Although it is easy for a person with a fairly wide experience to equip him or herself with as many serviceable backgrounds as he or she could possibly wish from that experience, still, if either or both of you, for any reason, feel these are not sufficient for your purposes, I urge you to compose completely new ones of your own devising. I agree with those who hold that any background the pleasured will approves can be added to the treasure house of memory for rhetorical use. Myself, I have found the November red of that Thanksgiving sky valuable and a pleasured way to bring to mind those figures approaching us from the bottom of the hill. I asked each of you if you objected to my letting go of the kite before they reached us. I still treasure your delight when my lighter burned through the kite's string and it leapt free.

Practice the pleasured sound of direct speech—some sweet invective for a caroling man: Some careful, sponsored song for our empire of last resort.

Arrangement

Arrangement

———✦———

I realize that my letter to you has now gone on at some length, longer perhaps than you would have liked. But my treatment of invention is now finished, and that is by far the most difficult part of the method. The remaining topics follow easily from what you have just read and have begun to practice for yourselves. Indeed, the other parts of this rhetoric will largely have been made familiar to you in the course of having undertaken the mastery of invention as I have presented it.

None of the family history documented here will have come as a surprise to you, I'm sure. Everything I have said you can easily verify from your own experience. But saying what happened is never enough. Among other difficult and delicate things, a place must be made for it in memory.

I trust you have been sufficiently diligent to reach this understanding for yourselves. Include, if you find it useful, some idea of the pleasure we took in flying the kite on Hospital Hill late that Thanksgiving afternoon.

Arrangement is the ordering and distribution of matter to be spoken, and making clear in your mind the place to which each thing is to be assigned. It can be divided into two parts—one concerns the ordered shape of the whole speech; the other, the shape of each of the individual arguments you will be using. Both parts should adhere to the principles I have already set forth: that is, for the overall structure of speech, the use of the introduction, statement of facts, division, proof of the division, refutation, and conclusion; and for each argument, the use of proposition, reason, proof of the reason, embellishment, and summary review. But there is another kind of arrangement, one in accordance with the specific circumstances of the occasion of speech. It is often necessary to employ changes and transpositions when the cause itself obliges you to modify with art the arrangement prescribed by the rules you have mastered. You may, for instance, suddenly need to convince your listeners of what it actually meant when Father used to say to AG and me that he never regretted having double majored in classics and math because, in combination, they had given him an intuitive, daily grasp of the disposition of force in international affairs.

When, from the trees bordering the golf course of Father's house in Maryland, I watched Ellen standing in the early spring light and thought she was about to burn, I made no move to stop her or to call out a warning in the pleasured air. It was Father who prevented the tragedy, and because of him, an ambulance came to take her to the hospital. As you know, Ellen continues to be close to Father and to other members of the family. A brief notice appeared in the local paper stating that an accident requiring an ambulance and emergency medical aid had occurred at 9:14 A.M. at the Calverton Road home of the President's special adviser for national security involving a guest who had been staying over the Easter holiday. Nothing further was mentioned concerning the incident, nor was there any follow-up. No national papers reported the story.

Practice arranging backgrounds, images, and arguments for an idea of an incident that had occurred earlier in the week. Father and I had fought as usual. My words were without weight of their own. Ellen was present and had interjected, "But what if Jarlath is right about the war?" Father turned to her and said softly, in a voice that seemed to hold within itself the pleasured violence of a burning field, "Do not speak of something you know nothing about. That is how all the damage is being done." I had repeated what a para-trooper, on his way back from three-months leave to re-port for a second tour of duty—he had requested his as-signment—had said to me, with perfect goodwill as we sat together on a bus: "You don't know what you're missing. You can get anything there you want. *Any-thing*." Father believed in the stewardship of absolute force. Moral men, he used to say, after all the words were done, had to prevail in a dangerous world.

Arrange some pleasured speech for the idea of Father drafting, and signing in the President's name, National Security Action Memorandum 328, dated 6 April 1965. Practice now arranging backgrounds, images, and arguments for the idea of him speaking it aloud, in a pleasured and Protestant style. He included no words to limit the new offensive role his order authorized: Subject to modifications in light of experience, to coordi-nation and direction in both capitals, the President approved an 18-20,000 man increase in U.S. military support forces to fill out existing units and supply needed logistic personnel. The President approved the deployment of two additional Marine Battalions and one Marine Air Squadron and associated headquarters and support elements. The President approved a change of mission for all Marine Battalions deployed there to permit their more active use under conditions to be established and approved by the Secretary of Defense in consultation with the Secretary of State. Air operation in Laos, particularly route-blocking operations in the Panhandle area, should be stepped up to the maximum remunerative rate. The President desires that with respect to these actions premature publicity be avoided by all possible precautions. The actions themselves should be taken as rapidly as practicable, but in ways that should minimize any appearance of sudden changes in policy, and official statements on these troop movements will be made only with the direct approval of the Secretary of Defense, in consultation with the Secretary of State. The President's desire is that these movements and changes should be understood as being gradual and wholly consistent with existing policy.

In the use of memory we can often encompass the record of an entire matter in one notation, with a single image. If you know the man concerned, picture him carefully as he is or was in the burning air. If he is not known to you, choose someone in your imagination to stand in for him, but do not use someone of the lowest class, so that you will be able to bring him to mind at once.

Practice some careful arrangement of obvious sound, some sweet invective for an idea of her pleasured burning: Caésar, I dó not cáre whéther your skín / is dárk or faír in thís bríght aír. / They sáy you líke my pléasured sóng and wánt / to máke it your ówn, párt of an infórmal admínistrative / stlýe. But whát sóund as áct can chánge / the pleásure táken / in this éndless / présent / despíte the súdden présence / of áll the clámoring déad?

Arrange some pleasured speech for an idea of Father descending in Asia. Use it as a background, where appropriate, but do not let the moveable metal staircase, placed against the plane's curving side, distract you from the smiling reasonableness of natural American rule. If your cause presents so great a difficulty that no one will be able to listen to an introduction with any patience, begin with a statement of facts and go back to the idea intended for your introduction in another place. If the statement of facts is not quite plausible, begin with some strong argument.

I held on to the photographs AG had given me for several years. My possession of them did not arise between us or with Father until AG began to be considered for more sensitive government positions within the Defense Department and also, I believe, within the National Security Administration. It was then that both Father and AG demanded them back, off-handedly at first and later with a determined and suddenly escalated insistence. Listening to each of them, I wondered if it always seems to children that fathers please themselves enormously.

To speak well, bring yourselves to have those feelings which you desire to instill in others. If you believe what you are saying, you will pronounce the words with a natural vehemence that is more beautiful and convincing than the rules of art, by themselves, can produce. Given Father's role in it, I do not see how to remember the war without an arrangement of speech concerning his pleasured will. I have retained for these purposes the image of three dogs loping that afternoon across Hospital Hill. I offer it to you here for your exercises and for verisimilitude.

We lived those years without speaking the family history all of us knew. It never occurred to us, whatever our strongest opinions concerning it, that we would ever have to. Father arranged in pleasured speech the following, upon which the government acted: We emphasize that our primary target in advocating a reprisal policy is the improvement of the situation in the *south*. Predictions of the effect of any given course of action upon the states of mind of people are difficult. It seems very clear that if we join in a policy of reprisal, there will be a sharp, immediate increase in optimism in the south among nearly all articulate groups. The Mission believes—and our own conversations confirm— that in all sectors of local opinion there is a strong belief that the United States could do much more if it would, and that they are suspicious of our failure to use more of our obviously enormous power. At least in the short run, the reaction to reprisal policy would be very favorable.

To represent the words to be remembered by images is an undertaking of great difficulty and should cause you to exercise your ingenuity all the more. Practice it in the following way, using the words Father, and now I, have given you above: For "Predictions of the effect of any given course of action upon the states of mind of people are difficult," place in the first background (the Buddhist monk being greeted happily upon his unexpected release) an image of a friend bringing you architectural plans of a gambling casino in which bets will be taken and odds given for a horse race in another city. Place in the casino a hanging mobile showing the earth in its orbit around the sun. Mark its center with a hand holding a written legal order disposing of the property of a deceased family member. This will give you "Predictions of the effect of any given course of action." In the second background (Father descending in Asia) place an image of a loud, rancorous argument among Westerners on the tarmac. Place on the head of each person a paper hat made from newspapers on which is dashed, in bright poster paint, an outline of the state from which he comes. This will give you, "Upon the states of mind of people are difficult."

This method of arrangement works only by the constant application of a practiced mind. The advantage of this method, however difficult it may appear at first, is that its discipline also frees the voice for the pleasure of invective: The son of a bitch over there who farts so dribblingly / burned the world and now insists on praise: / Father, what is it you want from us / Whose possibility you haven't already destroyed?

Arrange some pleasured speech for an idea of empire in this blue air; invent some German friend for an idea of him afterwards; compose some sweet invective now for the possible sound of another history.

In the proof and refutation of arguments use the following arrangement: place your strongest arguments at the beginning and the end of what you are saying; those of medium force, and those that are not useless but neither are they indispensable to the proof—that is, those that are weak when used by themselves but gain force when used together—place in the middle. The listener, immediately after hearing the statement of facts, wants to learn if the cause can be proved in some way. That is why the strongest argument should be presented first in a straightforward manner. For the

rest, that which is last heard is most easily committed
to memory. Therefore, when ceasing to speak, leave
some very strong argument in the hearer's mind. This
arrangement of topics in speaking, like arraying sol-
diers in battle, can bring you victory in your cause,
whether it be in judicial or deliberative matters, or in
praise or censure of prominent men.

In New Mexico, I saw Lena—who, I think, meant
more to Father than he could afford to let himself
know—stand up in the darkened room after Ernie
Glauber clicked the photograph of the thief's beheading
onto the screen. The scene had, he remarked, been pho-
tographed by an American foreign-service officer sta-
tioned in Peiping in 1904. Glauber had found it in the
State Department archives and wanted us to use it in
the documentary to illustrate the limits of repression in
shoring up a failing government's legitimacy. I saw her
stand and heard her say, "No. For you, any brown girl
will do." I cannot tell you what this means, but when I
mentioned it to her later, Lena could not remember having stood and was sure that, if she had, what she said
was, "I do not think this is an image we should use."
Despite my embarrassment, I nevertheless include this

incident here and propose it for your use in formal argument supporting the necessity of another, pleasured history.

As close as she is to him to this day, Lena, as far as I know, has never questioned Father directly about his responsibility for events between 1963 and 1965 or their aftermath.

Arrange some pleasured speech with backgrounds and arguments to give others an idea of Father's pleasured style: Joint reprisals would imply military planning in which the American role would necessarily be controlling, and this new relation should add to our bargaining power in other military efforts—and conceivably on a wider plane as well if a more stable government is formed. We have the whip hand in reprisals as we do not in other fields.

Each count of a charge being argued against someone should be placed in a different background successively, so that it can be held in the mind and retrieved at will in its proper order. The careful arrangement of backgrounds and the proper imprinting of the images allow for effortless calling to mind of whatever you wish.

Arrange some careful speech for an idea of the pleasured man singing his father's glory: If you are speaking of a city under siege and hold in your minds, for instance, the idea of Cholon burning, you may use either of two sets of topics—those based on considerations of security or those based on considerations of honor. If you wish to employ the topic of security for your purposes, you will say that nothing is more useful than safety; that no one can make use of virtue if he has not based his calculations on the idea of safety; that not even the gods help those who thoughtlessly put themselves in harm's way; that nothing honorable can be accomplished if there is not first the assurance of safety. If you wish to use the topic of honor, you will say that it is never proper to abandon the principle of virtue; that even pain, if that is what is feared, or death, if that is what is dreaded, is more tolerable than disgrace and infamy; that no one lives forever anyway and that the prospect of living in permanent shame is unbearable; that even if this present danger is evaded, there is no guarantee that another will not immediately or eventually take its place; that virtue extends even beyond death and that fortune, as is well known, favors the brave; that he who is safe for the moment is not necessarily a man living safely, nor is he who lives honorably necessarily he who lives safely; that he who lives shamelessly cannot be safe forever.

In his office I grabbed my father by the front of his white shirt and threatened him with harm. Security agents removed me before I could decide where or how to strike him. I was released immediately on Father's compassionate, unembarrassed order.

Nature herself teaches us how to practice so that we can hold things, even exact speech itself, in the mind. Events that are petty, ordinary, or banal we fail generally to remember because they are not novel or marvellous. But if we see or hear something that is exceptionally base, dishonorable, unbelievable, or laughable, then we are likely to remember it for a long time. This is the principle to follow in making your images: establish likenesses as striking as possible; have them doing something rather than being static; do not leave them vague; make them either exceptionally beautiful or singularly ugly; dress some of them in your mind in crowns or purple cloaks so that they will stand out better; or disfigure some by staining them with blood or soiling them with mud or assigning comic traits to their features. All this will help make it easier to call things readily to mind. The things we remember when they are real we likewise remember without difficulty when they are figments if they have been carefully delineated.

Practice arranging arguments in favor of some sound that includes the sudden presence of the querulous, ineffectual dead.

Practice some arrangement of speech, using your backgrounds, images, and ordered argument, favoring empire's pleasured rule. Be sure to include words for the sound of some court poet's honest invective against it. Produce from memory his song.

In the epideictic division of rhetoric there are two kinds of speech: praise and censure. The topics you use in giving praise therefore will also serve, by their contraries, as the basis for censure. Always to be considered are external circumstances, physical attributes, and qualities of character adjusted to the station of the person being described. Pay close attention, always, to the nature of the occasion. Remember that character depends upon judgment and reason and consists of the following: wisdom, justice, courage, temperance, and their contraries.

Arrange some sound in this bright air for an idea of his pleasured will; commmit to memory his words as pleasured acts. Father, Lena, and AG were all convinced that afternoon of the possibility that I might harm you. I do not claim they were only afraid that I would show you harmless, gruesome photographs. I wanted to fly kites with you to provide a background all of us could use should I prove successful in composing this short work of practical rhetoric that I will soon be sending off to you.

Arrange some pleasured speech for an idea of Father preparing these sentences in the Asian air for the President's signature: We want to keep before the enemy the carrot of our desisting as well as the stick of continued pressure. We also need to conduct the application of force so that there is always the prospect of worse to come.

Some believe that each word should be assigned an image so that it can easily be called to mind. Others, and I am among them, believe that each speaker should assign his or her own images, suitable to the particular circumstances and the actual occasion of their use, to groups of words which they wish to remember perfectly. The memorization of words themselves, while very difficult, is useful beyond what you might imagine. I strongly hold that the memorization of general matter is never enough.

Go over in your mind the images you have chosen for an idea of speech as direct address. Practice now some sweet invective of your own devising: Some good in this pleasured air / is loot for Marmurra now. / Caesar, how can you bear / to watch him swallow it like cum, / turning our sudden speech / into empire's endless gain?

Style

Style

—◆—

All disciplined speech falls into one of three registers of
style: the grand, the middle, or the simple. The simple is
used for subtlety and to prove the case; the middle, for
delight; the grand, for swaying hearers and making
your argument carry all the way to the back when
standing in front of a large audience.

Each register gains distinction from rhetorical figures. These should always be distributed sparingly, for
they set the style in sharp relief, and, just as with colors,
if packed in dense succession, they sow confusion. Be
careful to vary the styles within a given occasion of
speech. It is through variation that satiety in your listeners is most easily avoided.

Adopt a style with which to hold in memory the
party Father gave for AG the night before my brother
left for Asia. I asked AG at the end if Father had talked
to him. AG smiled. Father had repeated what Granny-
Dad had told him before he boarded a troop ship for

North Africa in 1942 at the age of twenty-three: "When everyone does his duty, nothing else needs to be said. Good luck, son, and God bless."

It is true that recent events are sometimes more difficult to discuss capably than those to which memory has given a distinctive and accomplished shape. In 1988, when AG was under consideration for a high government post—with the background checks and security clearances that come with Congressional over-sight—I threatened to use, against both him and Father, the photographs he had left with me. Sometime after Tet, I argued, they had to be shown. I was also prepar-ing, I told them, to testify without immunity concerning my role in 1983 in providing a democratic rationale for the killings our government had sponsored and some-times initiated in Nicaragua and El Salvador. I planned, I said, to offer the pictures and the use of the family name to some well-known journalist. I told Father and AG that I intended there to be publicity. That's why Father and AG came after us as we stood together that afternoon on Hospital Hill.

In any event, of course, the pictures were never made public, both for legal reasons and because of the media's lack of interest in the evidence I was offering them. Use all three registers—the simple, the middle, and the grand—for invective's sweet caress.

Style is the adoption of suitable words and sentences to the matter devised. But after you have learned the rules for a pleasured style—and practiced them—you will also need to know how to conceal your art. This is a necessary part of speaking's discipline. Listeners do not like to feel that they are being artificially played upon. They like examples of naturalness—like the Presidential tiepin the late beloved President had given him as a token of affection before he left for Dallas in 1963.

The grand style consists in the effortless and elegant arrangement of impressive words. A style closely akin to it, but a great fault, is the swollen style in which turgid, inflated language is used clumsily and in an affected manner. The middle style consists of words less elevated than those of the grand, but also not of the lowest, colloquial kind. The faulty style related to it is the slack or drifting one. It lacks sinews or joints to give it strength, precision, and agility. The simple style uses language tuned to the most current idiom of common speech. Father looked incredulous as I was holding him across the desk. Once, when he was angry, he made his voice a perfect instrument of his contempt by asking if I really thought that I was unmasking him, and, if I did, whether the method I had chosen would accomplish anything. It was my ineffectuality, he said, that truly disgusted him, ruling out any possible respect. The corresponding fault of style is the dry and bloodless— sometimes called the stunned or meagre—one.

You will not have realized how much it meant to me, when I worked in the library, to be aware that either or both of you might come in at any time to use it, and I would be able to see and talk with you. Des, do you remember the time you brought me the book with the Uccello painting? That was when I suddenly recognized I might be able to perfect a style with which to write to you about the family and the photographs AG had left with me. I sometimes thought of calling my method Some Speech for Father Descending in Asia: This Pleasure of Rule.

Practice a mixture of styles to give your hearers an idea of Father writing: The major necessary steps to be taken appear to us to be the following: We should complete the evacuation of dependents. We should quietly start the necessary westward deployments of [word illegible] contingency forces. We should develop and refine a running catalogue of the enemy's offenses which can be published regularly and related clearly to our own reprisals. Such a catalogue should perhaps build on the foundation of an initial White Paper.

That paper was never written. Practice using images and backgrounds for the memory of both the general matter and Father's exact words. Some claim that not all speech is memorable, but I strongly disagree. Backgrounds and images make it possible to preserve what is said among us so that it can be put to good use afterwards, if others agree. Father possessed the art of separating words from the necessity of act—of doing what, he said, everyone knew had to be done. There was a silence of effectiveness, he contended, that only the best men needed to know how to bear.

I write this now early in September 1996. Father is very ill. When young, I loved the way he wore his superiority as if it exempted him. I thought his pleasured will made him beautiful. Even in his present state, he is, it seems to me, inhabited by a kind of sordid, perfected grace.

To exhort you further in the matter of memory is not my intention. To do so would be to seem either to lack confidence in your dedication to the practice of this method or to have said less in this letter than the topic demands.

Employ a style of sweet invective, in which your hearers feel the images are about to come alive. Listeners should feel as if you were about to set your images free from the backgrounds you have provided them to mix promiscuously, almost without order or discipline. How far to go in this direction is not easy to recommend. As always, let yourselves be as attentive as possible to the nature of the occasion. There will always be stories and women, Father said, but you can never let yourself be trapped there. There can be no loss of will, no faltering, given the stakes, and the inherited sacrifice.

Distinction in a pleasured style is to be achieved through ornamentation using either figures of diction or figures of thought. It is a figure of diction if adornment is achieved through the polish of the language itself. A figure of thought lends distinction by the quality of the ideas it imparts to your speech independent of the words you choose to use. AG's career, as far as I know, has not been hurt by anything I have said or done.

Epanaphora, for instance, is a figure of diction in which the same word is used to form the beginning of phrases strung in quick succession to express either similar or contrasting ideas. For example: You dare to face the light? You dare to come into the sight of men? You dare to say a word? What can you say in your defense? Or: Have you not violated your oath? Have you not betrayed both your family and country? Have you not raised your hand against your father?

This figure has great charm, impressiveness, and force and should be used both for embellishment and amplification within a pleasured style.

Father is so sick that the drugs barely contain him. I moved to the Midwest just as I had planned; the job I mentioned has worked out. I live alone successfully and am content. I have returned to Northboro because Anna asked me to. Father's dying has simply gotten to be too much for her. Des, I have not seen Lena, nor do I expect to. Our silence has become permanent, I think, and mutual. I doubt meeting now would cause either of us any embarrassment.

When I saw Lena stand and speak in New Mexico, I thought I could feel the world breaking. No one, she told me, was more respected for his treatment of his staff than Father. The three of us should agree, I think, that in the beginning was the act. Des, there seemed to me to be so many people approaching us that afternoon on Hospital Hill because Lena was among them.

Adopt a pleasured, ornamented style, but do not neglect the art of invention in so doing. Practice committing to memory, using my backgrounds and images or your own, Father's words for administering a client state: We should initiate joint planning on both the civil and military level. Specifically, we should give a clear and strong signal to those now forming a government that we will be ready for this policy of sustained reprisal when they are.

Learn the virtues of invective's direct address: I wish I had told Father what was true, that I planned, in hell, to come and find him among all his unexpected dead.

Go over quickly in your mind, as often as necessary,

the parts and their order that this rhetoric contains. Keep in mind the sequence of the smaller sections from which the whole is made, the five fundamental units being: some rule or sound of speech, some piece of family history, some piece of admissible evidence, a memory technique, some example of direct address designed to impart fluency.

Go over, also, so that you can move among them quickly and as effortlessly as possible, the five photographs this method uses for backgrounds and the images I have placed within each of them. If you have substituted your own for mine by now, so much the better.

There is a certain repetition of words that is to be encouraged, not due to a poverty or lack of style, but because in repetition inheres an elegance which the ear can distinguish more easily than words can explain. Practice attending, for an instance, to what your ear hears in the sounds of a pleasured man saying: Some idea of her burning; this pleasure of rule.

Apostrophe is the figure of speech which expresses grief or indignation by means of an address to some man, or woman, or city, or place, or object, as, for example: Father, / from behind this modest / arrangement of stones, / I once could see a city not in flames. / If you don't believe me, / ask other people you once knew, / even in the midst of their pleasures, / if what I'm saying / isn't true.

If you use apostrophe sparingly and in its proper place, you will be able to instill in your hearers as much indignation as the occasion demands.

Sitting here, now, late in the year 1996, writing you and waiting for the next war—little or big—to begin, or even the war after that, it's easy to remember the pleasured feel of desperate speech and the abstract feel of the burning air. Father is dying. If you take nothing else from this method of direct address, take this possibility: that the possession of an ornamented style may be all you need. If ever you, too, should find it necessary to leave the family, consider that you may not have to wait for something more in order to speak.

Please remember that I was desperate then. I did, after all, attack my father as he sat working at his post. I reached across the wooden distance of his desk and briefly held the white, soft brightness of his shirt in my hands. But the point is to be able to speak capably concerning those things which law and custom have assigned to the uses of citizenship and to secure, as far as possible, the agreement of your hearers.

All authorities on this art include set pieces, adaptable to circumstances, on what is to be expected in the burning city at the hands of the enemy. Likewise, it is customary to include, for emulation, addresses to the jury excoriating the lack of sufficient pain to assign as punishment for the crime of parricide.

Practice some careful speech for another history, adopt an ornamented style. Do not neglect practicing the art of making images and keeping them memorable by assigning them exceptional beauty or by disfiguring them in some useful way. Use invective to make it possible to take a pleasured distance—both for yourself and for whomever is listening—on the cause you're arguing: Nóthing will stóp Cholón from búrning nów. / Caésar, for thís you ópened the wéstern lánds? / For thís you máke the Tágus Ríver / screám? / It's a mistáke to preténd / éveryone dóesn't nów dréam the dréams / your légions hád / sléeping péacefully on bóth bánks.

Practice a pleasured, ornamented style for an idea of Hospital Hill. If you don't find it too presumptuous, let the kite we flew together in that red sky on Thanksgiving afternoon carry the idea of my voice to you. Include in it, if you are willing, the photographs, wrapped in blue cloth, that I tried to find a way to give to you.

Hypophora is the figure of thought in which you inquire of your adversaries, or ask yourselves, what your adversaries can possibly say in their own favor, or what they can say against you. Then, you follow up with what ought or ought not to be said, given the circumstances as you have presented them. For example: I ask, therefore, from what source has the defendant become so wealthy? Has an ample patrimony been left him? Has some relative's bequest come down to him? That cannot be argued. In fact, he has been disinherited and denounced by his entire family and all his friends. Or: I have observed that numerous defendants look for support in some honorable deed which not even their enemies can impeach. Will he take refuge in his father's name and virtue? How can he? By the laws he himself took an oath to defend, he has condemned himself to death and public ignominy.

General, on Hospital Hill, you said that I spoke as if I wished that I had gone to the war instead of your father. It's true, I often wish both that I had gone with him and that he had stayed away from it with me. I dreamt recently of that fifth photograph of AG and his men. In the dream I am the one kneeling, holding up the necklace of ears. The feeling is of some great happiness about to be revealed.

Practice a careful, ornamented style for an idea of Father writing: We should *not* now accept the idea of negotiations of any sort. A program of sustained reprisal will not involve us in nearly the level of international recrimination which would be precipitated by a go-North program. For this reason the international pressures for negotiation should be quite manageable.

I realize I have taken up a great deal of your time by now. I have taken close to as many years composing this as your ages when I started. Perhaps enough has been said, but let me briefly turn to delivery, or some might rightly accuse me of having neglected the most important part of all. Father is dying and cannot remember anything. There is only presence, endless need, and no urgency. There is lack of continence. Somehow he retains his dignity. It is as if only his gracefulness has not forsaken him—as if it still remembers and inhabits him.

He is a gentleman, the woman says who cares for him. She is his favorite of three. I have tried to limit myself here to what might prove useful in helping you address necessary matters of family history.

Delivery

$\mathcal{D}$e*livery*

———⊷◆⊶———

Delivery, with good reason, has been called the most important part of rhetoric. Delivery is the graceful regulation of voice, demeanor, and gesture—a way of creating presence out of air. Only a practiced rule of rhetoric will allow you to retain for immediate use words, ideas, events, and their arrangement and to pass them on effectively as speech, suitable again for memory. Only rhetoric and its history have a very close relationship to private and public affairs and can ensure the safe protection of oneself and one's friends. Delivery may be divided into two parts, gesture and sound. Quality of voice should be perfected with respect to flexibility, volume, and stability. Do not rely upon the family's privilege and exemption when you speak. It helps if you imagine some sound for the feel of careful speech leaving the warm opening of the mouth.

Sharp exclamation injures the voice and likewise jars the hearer. It imparts awkwardness to the occasion, belonging more to the world of feminine outcry than to the dignity of forceful speech. Flexibility of voice has three aspects: the conversational tone, the tone of debate, and the tone of amplification. The latter's function is to rouse the hearer to anger or pity.

For the narrative, conversational tone, varied intonations are necessary so that we seem to recount everything just as it took place. Learn to do good. Memorize what has been said in order to know what is true. Adopt a new and easy sweetness of tone for an idea of it afterwards. Invent some pleasured speech to recount an event of family history accurately.

Your delivery should be fairly rapid when you narrate that which was done with force, slower when you speak of things done in a more leisurely fashion. If in the statement of facts there occur any declarations, demands, replies, or exclamations of astonishment, you should give careful attention to expressing with your voice the feelings and thoughts of the personage your speech concerns.

It is one thing to acquire the art of direct address and another to make use of it through the art of delivery.

Do not use up the brilliance of the voice in one loud outburst. A calm tone in the introduction is useful for the voice's stability.

We cannot choose our fathers, but it is our responsibility to imagine them. Sharp exclamation injures the voice and likewise jars the hearer.

The conversational tone is divided into four aspects: the dignified, the explicative, the narrative, and the facetious. The narrative is to be cultivated so as to impart to your listener a convincing account of events that have occurred or might have occurred. The tone of amplification is divided into two aspects: the hortatory and the pathetic. The hortatory is to be used to emphasize a fault or to incite a listener's indignation. The pathetic is to be used to amplify misfortune and thereby to win over a listener to pity. The tone of debate is divided into the sustained and the broken.

For the dignified conversational tone you will need to use the full throat, but employ the calmest, most subdued voice possible, without stooping to histrionics.

Without empire and the pleasured will, what possible fulfillment for the citizen? Some sound for the pleasure of rule in this New World. For the broken tone of debate, shoot out one arm laterally very quickly, pace up and down, stop and stomp the right foot occasionally. Peer about you with a piercing, fixed, and determined expression. As if speech, or fire, could take the place of burning skin and make its discarded pleasure sing.

For the pathetic tone of amplification, it is appropriate to slap your thigh and strike your head with your open hand, alternating these gestures with the resigned calmness of deliberate movements, yet with a disturbed expression on your face. I do realize, of course, what a difficult task I have undertaken here—to convey in writing the movements of the body and the sound of the voice speaking its pleasure.

Father's health has worsened over the past few days. Everything grows less familiar to him. His confusion seems limitless. Some days are better, a little, than others. There is now very little time, the doctors think. Dead family members come back to him in the hall of a house he remembers from childhood that I have never seen. I have held onto this letter probably for too long. I will make copies soon and send them, one for each of you, and one to Elizabeth. The original I will keep in case either of you, or I myself, should ever require it.

Everyone, he once said, owed, when required, the state a life. The best men, he thought, had the responsibility to rule without restraint. He committed crimes against humanity. This is documented. I have been a disloyal son and committed treason, the evidence could be made to show.

The actual event can lose its independent value. An abstruse art of allegorical exegesis is born whenever this occurs. Invent some speech for the pleasured man's burning.

As you become practiced in this method, remember to allow yourselves freedom to depart from adherence to its exact prescriptions.

Remember that the windpipe is injured when filled suddenly with violent outbursts of sound and that it is rested by silence. Do not hesitate to employ long pauses, especially when you are using the conversational tone. Toward the close of speaking, it is perfectly proper to deliver long passages of sound in one unbroken breath. The throat is warm and the voice has been restored by your use of all the tones of address.

I recommend that you refrain from committing to writing anything you do not intend to memorize and use in some manner of direct address. Your body should be unencumbered when you speak. Good men, he said, should rule. Anything else, history showed, was abdication of responsibility and an invitation to the worst, who are always present. Evil was limitless. The doctrine of natural depravity, he maintained, was empirically verified and a precious inheritance.

Unlike stability of voice, flexibility depends entirely upon adherence to rhetorical rules. The tone of conversation should be relaxed and close to common speech. The tone of debate should be excited, equally suited as it is to vehement proof and vehement refutation. There will need to be some speech afterwards for the way empire penetrates the skin.

Because I do not know when I will be back East again, I have been to check on the condition of Father's house in Maine to see if it needed anything. While I was there, I walked the old logging road he always used to walk. A little way in, I found the dessicated remnants of a young porcupine lying in the sun, and I suddenly knew I was free to release my argument. I don't pretend to understand why seeing the ground through its blackened strips of skin made me eloquent, but it did: some careful speech for an idea of him.

Preserve in memory the evidence against him, and do not neglect the pleasured uses of invective. General, as you know, I and your father are hopelessly estranged. I would like to think that I wish him no ill.

When discussing delivery, it is necessary to pay close attention to the body's physical movements. The body must move so as to increase the plausibility of what you say. Be careful not to go too far either on the side of elegance or vulgarity. Remember you are not an actor on stage. For the conversational, explicative tone, lean forward and bring your face as close to your listeners as possible, since this is the way to prove something conclusively or get someone to act on what you say. For the pathetic tone of amplification, combine slow and graceful—sometimes halting—gestures with a sad and wounded expression and a calm, even tone of voice for the strongest effect.

Father signed the memorandum authorizing offensive action on the part of U.S. troops in the President's name, 6 April 1965. I am confident now of my trust in you especially because I am not aware of having omitted any of the rules of rhetoric from what I have written here.

If I do not hear from either of you, I will understand. Silence, according to this method, is also a way of speaking. And if you want to ask me in person what it is I have been doing all these years, perhaps I will ask your permission to say aloud a little of what I have written here. I will begin anywhere and proceed for as long as I can manage from memory.

Note

Jarlath Lanham's method—and mine—are greatly in the debt of Harry Caplan's meticulous, graceful, and, to a nonclassicist's limited discernment, inexhaustible erudition on rhetorical matters. These are displayed by his 1954 translation of *Ad C. Herennium; De Ratione Dicendi*, published as the first volume in the Loeb Classical Library edition of the works of Cicero. Erroneously attributed to Cicero from the time of Jerome until the early Renaissance, this work, by an unknown author, is from the first century B.C. and the oldest suriving complete Latin rhetoric.

Gratefully acknowledged also is the assistance provided by two other translators, Horace Gregory and James Michie, who both accomplished the dauntingly difficult task of rendering the voice of Catullus into lyrical English. Their editions of that great poet of empire's words are identically titled *The Poems of Catullus;* Gregory's translation was originally published as a dual language edition by Covici-Friede in 1931, then in English only by Grove Press in 1956; Michie's edition was published by Random House in 1969.

The evidence Jarlath brings against his father is taken verbatim from *The Pentagon Papers.*

DALKEY ARCHIVE PAPERBACKS

FELIPE ALFAU, *Chromos.*
  Locos.
  Sentimental Songs.
ALAN ANSEN,
  Contact Highs: Selected Poems 1957-1987.
DJUNA BARNES, *Ladies Almanack.*
  Ryder.
JOHN BARTH, *LETTERS.*
  Sabbatical.
ANDREI BITOV, *Pushkin House.*
ROGER BOYLAN, *Killoyle.*
CHRISTINE BROOKE-ROSE, *Amalgamemnon.*
GERALD BURNS, *Shorter Poems.*
MICHEL BUTOR,
  Portrait of the Artist as a Young Ape.
JULIETA CAMPOS, *The Fear of Losing Eurydice.*
ANNE CARSON, *Eros the Bittersweet.*
LOUIS-FERDINAND CÉLINE, *Castle to Castle.*
  North.
  Rigadoon.
HUGO CHARTERIS, *The Tide Is Right.*
JEROME CHARYN, *The Tar Baby.*
EMILY HOLMES COLEMAN, *The Shutter of Snow.*
ROBERT COOVER, *A Night at the Movies.*
STANLEY CRAWFORD,
  Some Instructions to My Wife.
RENÉ CREVEL, *Putting My Foot in It.*
RALPH CUSACK, *Cadenza.*
SUSAN DAITCH, *Storytown.*
PETER DIMOCK,
  A Short Rhetoric for Leaving the Family.
COLEMAN DOWELL, *Island People.*
  Too Much Flesh and Jabez.
RIKKI DUCORNET, *The Fountains of Neptune.*
  The Jade Cabinet.
  Phosphor in Dreamland.
  The Stain.

WILLIAM EASTLAKE, *Lyric of the Circle Heart.*
STANLEY ELKIN, *The Dick Gibson Show.*
ANNIE ERNAUX, *Cleaned Out.*
LAUREN FAIRBANKS, *Muzzle Thyself.*
  Sister Carrie.
LESLIE A. FIEDLER,
  Love and Death in the American Novel.
RONALD FIRBANK, *Complete Short Stories.*
FORD MADOX FORD, *The March of Literature.*
JANICE GALLOWAY, *Foreign Parts.*
  The Trick Is to Keep Breathing.
WILLIAM H. GASS,
  Willie Masters' Lonesome Wife.
C. S. GISCOMBE, *Giscome Road.*
  Here.
KAREN ELIZABETH GORDON, *The Red Shoes.*
GEOFFREY GREEN, ET AL, *The Vineland Papers.*
PATRICK GRAINVILLE, *The Cave of Heaven.*
JOHN HAWKES, *Whistlejacket.*
ALDOUS HUXLEY, *Antic Hay.*
  Point Counter Point.
  Those Barren Leaves.
  Time Must Have a Stop.
TADEUSZ KONWICKI, *The Polish Complex.*
EWA KURYLUK, *Century 21.*
OSMAN LINS,
  The Queen of the Prisons of Greece.
ALF MAC LOCHLAINN,
  The Corpus in the Library.
  Out of Focus.
D. KEITH MANO, *Take Five.*
BEN MARCUS, *The Age of Wire and String.*
DAVID MARKSON, *Collected Poems.*
  Reader's Block.
  Springer's Progress.
  Wittgenstein's Mistress.
CARL R. MARTIN, *Genii Over Salzburg.*

Visit our website at www.cas.ilstu.edu/english/dalkey/dalkey.html

DALKEY ARCHIVE PAPERBACKS

Visit our website at www.cas.ilstu.edu/english/dalkey/dalkey.html

Dalkey Archive Press
ISU Campus Box 4241, Normal, IL 61790–4241
fax (309) 438–7422